Challah!

Words & Pictures by **Ellen Kahan Zager**

Ellen Kahan Zager
1220 Bank St. #410
Baltimore, Maryland 21202
410-484-9110

etsy.com/shop/ekzcreative

Ordering Information:
Quantity sales. Special discounts are available on quantity purchases by schools, not for profit organizations, book stores and others. For details, contact the publisher at the address above.

Printed in the United States of America

Publisher's Cataloging-in-Publication data
Zager, Ellen Kahan.
Challah! / Ellen Kahan Zager.

ISBN: 979-0-578-23259-1
1. Children's fiction 2. Jewish 3. A story about Shabbat.
4. Jewish family 5. Shabbat rituals I. Zager, Ellen Kahan
II. Challah!

9780578232591

for my beloved Elior Jesse, the inspiration for this book.

Challah?

Challah?

Challah?

Challah?

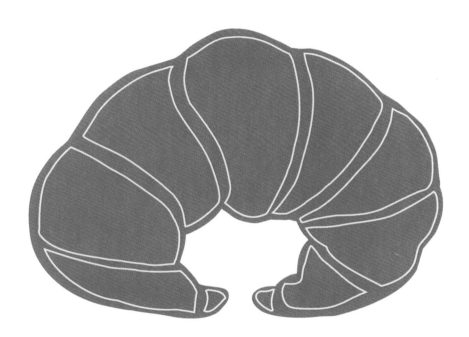

Challah?

Challah?

Challah!

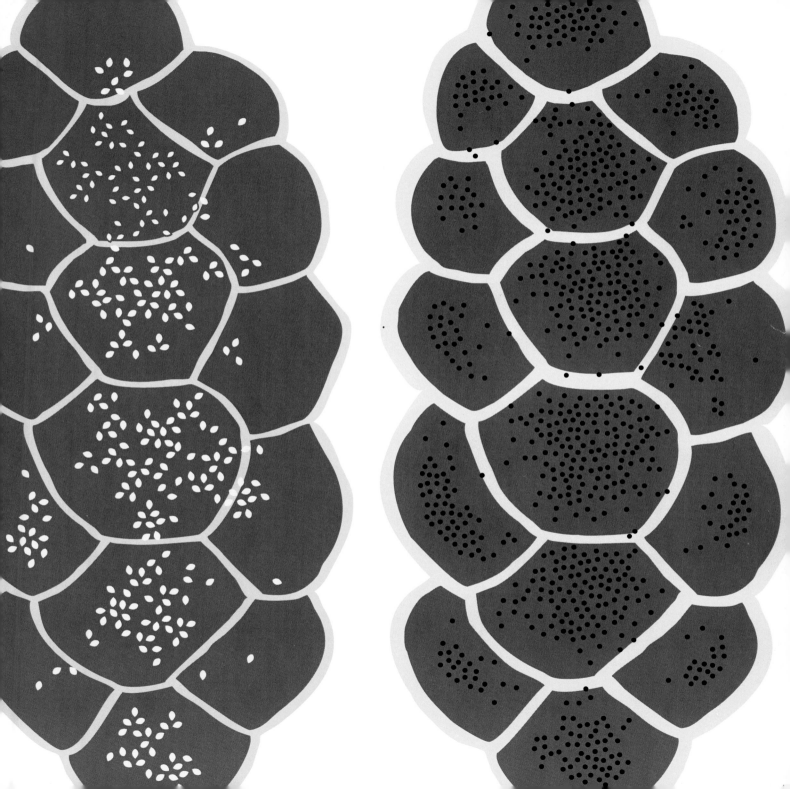

Shabbat Shalom!

Blessings for Shabbat

Blessing when we light the candles

בָּרוּךְ אַתָּה ה׳, אֱלֹהֵינוּ מֶלֶךְ הָעוֹלָם, אֲשֶׁר קִדְּשָׁנוּ בְּמִצְוֹתָיו וְצִוָּנוּ לְהַדְלִיק נֵר שֶׁל שַׁבָּת:

Bah-rooch Ah-tah Ah-doh-nahy, Eh-loh-hay-noo Meh-lehch hah-oh-lahm, ah-shehr keed-shah-noo beh-meets-voh-tahv veh-tsee-vah-noo leh-hahd-leek nehr shehl Shah-baht.

Blessed are You, God, Ruler of the Universe, Who has provided us with a path to holiness through the observance of mitzvot and has instructed us to kindle the Shabbat lights.

Kiddush (Blessing over the wine)

בָּרוּךְ אַתָּה ה׳, אֱלֹהֵינוּ מֶלֶךְ הָעוֹלָם בּוֹרֵא פְּרִי הַגָּפֶן.

Bah-rooch Ah-tah Ah-doh-nahy, Eh-loh-hay-noo Meh-lehch hah-oh-lahm, boh-reh pree hah-gah-fehn.

Blessed are You, God, Ruler of the Universe, Who creates fruit of the vine.

Motsi (Blessing over the challah)

בָּרוּךְ אַתָּה ה׳, אֱלֹהֵינוּ מֶלֶךְ הָעוֹלָם הַמּוֹצִיא לֶחֶם מִן הָאָרֶץ.

Bah-rooch Ah-tah Ah-doh-nahy, Eh-loh-hay-noo Meh-lehch hah-oh-lahm, hah-moh-tsee leh-chehm meen hah-ah-rehts.

Blessed are You, God, Ruler of the Universe, Who brings forth bread from the earth.

Blessings over children

יְשִׂימְךָ אֱלֹהִים כְּאֶפְרַיִם וְכִמְנַשֶּׁה.

Yeh-seem-chah Eh-loh-heem keh-Ehf-rah-yeem veh-chee-Meh-nah-sheh.

May God make you like Efraim and Menashe.

יְשִׂימֵךְ אֱלֹהִים כְּשָׂרָה, רִבְקָה, רָחֵל וְלֵאָה.

Yeh-see-mehch Eh-loh-heem keh-Sah-rah, Reev-kah, Rah-chehl veh-Leh-ah.

May God make you like Sarah, Rebecca, Rachel and Leah.

יְבָרֶכְךָ ה׳ וְיִשְׁמְרֶךָ. יָאֵר ה׳ פָּנָיו אֵלֶיךָ וִיחֻנֶּךָּ. יִשָּׂא ה׳ פָּנָיו אֵלֶיךָ וְיָשֵׂם לְךָ שָׁלוֹם.

Yeh-vah-reh-cheh-chah Ah-doh-nahy veh-yeesh-meh-reh-chah.
Yah-ehr Ah-doh-nahy pah-nahv eh-leh-chah vee-choo-neh-kah.
Yee-sah Ah-doh-nahy pah-nahv eh-leh-chah veh-yah-sehm leh-chah shah-lohm.

May God bless you and guard you.
May God shine God's face on you and be gracious to you.
May God turn God's face to you and grant you peace.

Ellen Kahan Zager is a graphic designer, writer, poet, and creative consultant. Most important of all, she is Elior Jesse's grandma. She's mom to Sara and Sara's two siblings Laura and David, wife to Jack (Zee) and daughter of Ann Hettleman Kahan (Gigi) and Sammy Kahan of blessed memory. A third generation Baltimorean, her great grandpa Kalman Hettleman began a scrap metal business in 1904 "after getting off the boat at Ft. McHenry". Ellen is a proud Zionist and has been an advocate for Jewish education for decades. She tutors Baltimore City elementary school children in reading and Israeli high school students in English (over the internet). She enjoys many, many hobbies, most of all reading, swimming and playing the piano.

JENNIFER BISHOP